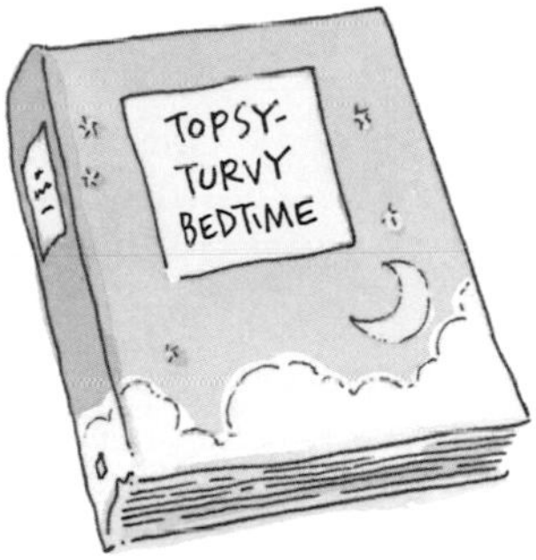
TOPSY-
TURVY
BEDTIME

This one is for Jessica and Elijah
J. L.

For Amaya, Braden, and Ella
T. A.

Text copyright © 2008 by Joan Levine
Illustrations copyright © 2008 by Tony Auth

First edition 2008

Library of Congress Cataloging-in-Publication Data is available.

Library of Congress Catalog Card Number pending

ISBN 978-0-7636-3008-9

2 4 6 8 10 9 7 5 3 1

Printed in China

This book was typeset in Myriad Tilt.
The illustrations were done in watercolor.

Candlewick Press
2067 Massachusetts Avenue
Cambridge, Massachusetts 02140

visit us at www.candlewick.com

Topsy-Turvy
Bedtime

Joan Levine

illustrated by Tony Auth

CANDLEWICK PRESS
CAMBRIDGE, MASSACHUSETTS

Once upon a time, there was a little girl named Arathusela. She lived in Brooklyn with her mother and father.

Every night, Arathusela put up a terrible fuss about going to bed.

"I wish I could go to sleep now," said her father.

"You do?" asked Arathusela, surprised that anyone would wish to go to sleep.

"Yes, we love to go to sleep and get our rest," said her mother.

"Well, then," said Arathusela, "why don't you let me put you to sleep for a change?"

"Fine," said her father.

"Marvelous," said her mother.

Arathusela went to finish putting her dolls to sleep.

Her mother and father began to watch the news.

"Time for bed, you two," said Arathusela.

"What? We're right in the middle of our favorite
show!" cried her parents.

"I'm sorry," said Arathusela, "but it's time for bed.
Now go and get into your pajamas. I don't want
to hear any fuss!"

"Just a few more minutes?" asked her mother.

"Absolutely not," said Arathusela.

Her parents got into their nightclothes.

"Did you brush your teeth?"

"Not yet," said her parents.

"Well, go and brush your teeth, and then I will read you a story."

Her parents brushed their teeth.

"Well?" asked Arathusela. "Have you decided what book you would like to hear?"

"It's my turn to pick," said her mother.
"No, it's my turn," said her father.

"You always get your way," said her mother.
"No, you always get *your* way," said her father.

"That's it. I will pick out the book," said Arathusela.

"I'm sure we will all enjoy this one.

Can you both see the pictures?"

"Yes," said her mother.

"Could you move it over a little more?" said her father.

"Is this all right?" asked Arathusela.

"That's fine," they both said together.

When she finished the book, Arathusela said,
"Time for bed. Did you go to the toilet?"
"No," said her mother.
"No," said her father.
"Well, go, then," said Arathusela.

Both parents went to the toilet.

"I want something to drink," said her father.

"You may have water, juice, or milk," said Arathusela.

"I want soda," said her mother.

"There is no soda at bedtime," said Arathusela.

"But I want some," her father whined.

"I don't think you two want anything to drink. You're just overtired and carrying on."

"I'll have some orange juice," her father said with a sigh.

"So will I," said her mother.

"All right," said Arathusela after they had finished their juice. "Time for bed."

Arathusela's parents climbed into their bed.

"I want a kiss," said her mother.

"Me too," said her father.

"I want a hug," said her father.

"Me too," said her mother.

Arathusela gave them each a hug.

"We forgot to kiss and hug you back,"

said her mother.

"You forgot to sing us a song," her father said.

"OK," said Arathusela. "But that's it. I'm losing my patience."

Arathusela sang:

"Rock-a-bye, baby, on the treetop.

When the wind blows, the cradle will rock.

When the bough breaks, the cradle will fall,

And down will come baby, cradle and all."

"Good night," she whispered as she left the room.

She had just closed the door when she heard,

"Arathusela, Arathusela."

Arathusela pushed open the door and yelled,

"I've had it!

I'm on the brink!

This is the last straw.

You're asking for it.

WHAT IS IT?"

"Please leave the door open," said her father in a very little voice.

"OK," grumbled Arathusela.

She went into her room.

Her dolls were still asleep.

She made some snakes and pancakes with her clay.

She played with her felt pens and paper.

Then she went into the living room,
where her parents sat when she went to
sleep. There was not much to do there.

Arathusela was lonesome.

She walked back to her parents' room.

"What is it?" asked her mother.

"Can I sleep with you?" asked Arathusela.

"Absolutely not," said her father.

"Hey, wait a minute. I'm the boss tonight," said Arathusela.

"Move over!"

And she climbed into her parents' bed, and
they all snuggled down and went to sleep.